Biblical Characters and Words A-Z Alphabet Books

Sheila Latimore

ISBN: 979-8-89397-535-2

Edition: First

Published by EliteScribes Book Writing

Dedication

I dedicate this book to my late grandmother, Rosie Smith, who always believed in me and took me to church every chance she could. Some of my most cherished memories are of teaching her how to write her name and how to read. From the time I was a little girl and well into my teenage years, I would sit with her, reading the Bible together. Those moments not only deepened my faith but also ignited my passion for education.

Acknowledgements

First and foremost, I want to thank God—the Father, the Son, and the Holy Spirit—for granting me the wisdom and courage to write this book. I am deeply grateful to my daughter, Santana Latimore, for always standing by my side as my unwavering supporter. My heartfelt thanks go to my sisters, Earnestine Derico and Brenda Stovall, for their constant belief in me and their encouragement to keep moving forward. I also want to express my deepest gratitude to my late mother, Classie Jones, whose words of wisdom inspired me to strive for excellence in all things. Finally, I extend my sincere appreciation to my church family, friends, and colleagues for their support and prayers.

In advance, I want to express my heartfelt thanks to everyone who embraces the messages within this book. I ray that God opens your eyes to His Word and grants you the understanding He desires for you to receive.

Preface

From the dawn of creation to the final revelation, the Bible is rich with stories of individuals whose lives serve as testimonies of faith, resilience, and divine purpose. This book is inspired by the legacy of these men and women—each one a symbol of God's enduring promise and the power of unwavering belief.

Beginning with **Adam**, the first man created in God's image, we witness the birth of humanity and the consequences of choice. Then comes **Abraham**, the father of faith, whose obedience laid the foundation for generations to come. Moving forward, **David**, the shepherd boy turned king, shows us the power of repentance and a heart devoted to God, while **Deborah**, the fearless judge, demonstrates the strength and wisdom of a woman led by the Spirit.

For every letter, there is a name, a story, a purpose. From **Esther**, who risked her life for her people, to **Elijah**, who called down fire from heaven in bold faith, the Bible showcases not just characters, but pillars of divine intervention. **Moses** led a nation out of bondage, while **Mary**, the mother of Jesus, embraced her calling with grace and humility.

Even in the shadows of betrayal, like with **Judas**, or in moments of redemption, like **Paul**, the narrative remains one of transformation and hope. **Ruth** teaches loyalty, **Solomon** exemplifies wisdom, and **Zacchaeus** shows the power of redemption through a single encounter with Christ.

This is more than a collection of stories; it is a journey through the alphabet of faith—a testament that in every season, God is present, guiding, redeeming, and restoring.

Welcome to the journey, from A to Z.

A

Abraham

And he believed in the LORD, and He accounted it to him for righteousness. (Genesis 15:6) Neither shall thy name any more be called Abram, but thy name shall be Abraham; for a father of many nations have I made thee. (Genesis 17:5)

B

Boaz

So, Boaz took Ruth, and she was his wife; and when he went in unto her,
the LORD gave her conception and she bore a son. (Ruth 4:13)

C

Cornelius

There was a certain man in Caesarea called Cornelius, a centurion of the band called the Italian Band, a devout man and one who feared God with all his house, who gave many alms to the people and prayed to God always. (Acts 10:1-2)

D

Daniel

Now when Daniel knew that the writing was signed, he went into his house; and his windows being open in his chamber toward Jerusalem, he kneeled upon his knees three times a day, and prayed and gave thanks before his God, as he did formerly. (Daniel 6:10)

E

Elizabeth

Elizabeth was the wife of Zechariah and the mother of John the Baptist. Also, the cousin of Mary Jesus' mother. (Luke1:6)

F

Father

As a father pitieth his children, so the LORD pitieth them that fear Him.
(Psalms 103:13)

H

Hosea

Hosea took Gomer for a wife. (Hosea 1:3). Hosea took Gomer as wife because the Lord to him to as a symbol of how God married to the backsliders.

I

Israel

"For thou art a holy people unto the LORD thy God; the LORD thy God hath chosen thee to be a special people unto Himself, above all people that are upon the face of the earth. (Deuteronomy 7:6)

J

Joseph

Now Israel loved Joseph more than all his children, because he was the son of his old age; and he made him a coat of many colors. (Genesis 37:3)

K

Keturah

Abraham second wife after the death of Sarah. (Genesis 25:1-2)

L

Laban

Laban promised his younger daughter Rachel to Jacob in return for seven years' service, only to trick him into marrying his elder daughter Leah instead. Jacob then served another seven years in exchange for the right to marry his choice, Rachel, as well. (Genesis 29:18)

M

Moses

God gave Moses the ten commandments when he was on Mount Sinai.
(Genesis 19:25)

N

Nathan

And it came to pass, when the king sat in his house and the LORD had given him rest roundabout from all his enemies, that the king said unto Nathan the prophet, "See now, I dwell in a house of cedar, but the ark of God dwelleth within curtains. (2 Samuel 7:1-2)

O

Obadiah

And Azel had six sons whose names are these: Azrikam, Bocheru, and Ishmael, and Sheariah, and Obadiah, and Hanan. All these were the sons of Azel. (1 Chronicles 8:38)

P

Peter

In a vision, Peter, saw all types of animals; The Lord commanded him to kill and eat. Peter refused saying they were unclean. (Acts 10: 10-16)

Q

Queen Sheba

And when the queen of Sheba heard of the fame of Solomon concerning the name of the LORD, she came to test him with hard questions. (1 Kings 10:1)

R

Ruth

And she went, and came and gleaned in the field after the reapers; and she happened to light on a part of the field belonging unto Boaz, who was of the kindred of Elimelech. (Ruth 2:3)

S

Sarah

Sarah was Abraham first wife. For Sarah conceived and bore Abraham a son in his old age, at the set time of which God had spoken to him. And Abraham called the name of his son who was born unto him, whom Sarah bore to him, Isaac. (Genesis 21:1-3)

T

Timothy

Unto Timothy, my own son in the faith: Grace, mercy, and peace from God our Father and Jesus Christ our Lord. (1 Timothy 1:1)

U

Uriah

Uriah was a man of valor who fought for Israel and he was the husband of Bathsheba. (2 Samuel 11:3)

V

Queen Vashti

The King Ahasuerus wants to show of Queen Vashti to the people and prince because of her beauty but she refused. (Esther 1:10-12)

W

Wisemen

King Herod inquired of the wisemen where to find baby Jesus. (Matthew 2: 7-8)

X

King Xerxes

King Xerxes was another name for King Ahasuerus. (Esther 3:11)

Y

Yeshua

Jesus was called Yeshua which Hebrew means salvation. (Psalms 14:7)

Z

Zechariah

Zechariah was the husband of Elizabeth and the father of John the
Baptist. Luke1:67-79

About the Author

Sheila Latimore has faithfully served as an elder in the House of God since 2012. She is both an educator and a veteran, with a deep passion for children and the elderly. With over sixteen years of experience in education and eight years of service in the military, her life has been marked by excitement and challenges that, with God's guidance, she has been able to overcome. Born and raised in Montgomery, Alabama, she is the second oldest of six siblings.

This is more than a collection of stories; it is a journey through the alphabet of faith—a testament that in every season, God is present, guiding, redeeming, and restoring.